Fairy Tale Twists

For my beautiful niece, Summer,
who loves peas.
K.D.

For Tina
M.B.

Reading Consultant: Prue Goodwin, Lecturer in literacy and children's books

ORCHARD BOOKS
338 Euston Road, London NW1 3BH
Orchard Books Australia
Level 17/207 Kent Street, Sydney, NSW 2000

First published in 2012
First paperback publication in 2013

ISBN 978 1 40831 211 7 (hardback)
ISBN 97 8 1 40831 219 3 (paperback)

Text © Katie Dale 2012
Illustrations © Matt Buckingham 2012

A CIP catalogue record for this book is available
from the British Library.

1 3 5 7 9 10 8 6 4 2 (hardback)
3 5 7 9 10 8 6 4 2 (paperback)

Printed in Great Britain

Orchard Books is a division of Hachette Children's Books,
an Hachette UK company.

www.hachette.co.uk

Fairy Tale
Twists
Goldilocks and the Pea

Written by Katie Dale
Illustrated by Matt Buckingham

ORCHARD

Long ago, or so I'm told,
there lived a girl with hair like gold.
So fair were Gretel's curly locks
that she was nicknamed "Goldilocks".

She lived with Hansel – her twin brother,
and their dad, and new stepmother.
Till one day their father died,
and left the twins with his new bride…

…who cooked the most disgusting food!
Said Goldilocks: "Don't think me rude,
but *must* we *always* dine on greens?
I can't stand cabbage, peas or beans.
They're horrible – I've had enough!"
"Oh really?" said her stepmum. "Tough!"

"Well, thanks a bundle," Hansel moaned,
as both their hungry tummies groaned.

"Don't worry, bro – I've brought some
bread!"

"Hurray! I'm starving!" Hansel said.

"It's not to eat – it's hard as nails!
But look, let's use the crumbs as trails.
That way, wherever we may roam,
we'll always find our way back home."

The twins walked deep into the wood
to find whatever food they could.

Hans found some berries, bright and red.
"Not ripe enough," his sister said.

And then some mushrooms –
  "Nope," said Goldy.
"*Look* at them – they're old and mouldy!"

Cherries, figs and hazelnuts
all met with sighs and groans and tuts.

At last poor Hans could take no more.

They'd searched for hours, his feet were sore.

But most of all, his tummy hurt.

He grabbed an apple caked in dirt.

"Hans, wait! That's filthy!"

 "*I don't care!*"

cried hungry Hansel in despair.

"I'm starving, sis – I need a snack!

There's no food here – I'm going back!"

But when he turned and looked around…
no crumbs were left upon the ground!
"The pigeon ate them!" Goldy cried.
"Lucky pigeon!" Hansel sighed.
"We're lost!" wailed Goldy in dismay.
"However will we find our way?"

The night grew dark, the wind blew chill,
they searched around in vain – until
a sweet aroma filled the breeze.
They followed it between the trees…

And came across a path that led
straight to a house of – gingerbread!
Cried Hansel, "It's a dream come true!
The doorbell is a penny chew!"

"Hang on!" cried Goldy. "Hansel, wait!"
I cannot find the eat-by date!"
But Hansel ran ahead, all smiles.
"There's even choc-chip cookie tiles!"

The cottage door burst open wide.
"Oh, children! Welcome! Come inside!"
The old hag smiled. "I've sweets and cake –
come help yourself! I love to bake!"

Young Hansel raced straight through
    the door,
but Goldy wasn't quite so sure.
The hag looked creepy, and, I mean,
a house of sweets was hardly clean!

Just then there came a **BANG** and **CRASH**
followed by a blinding **FLASH!**
Then suddenly – quick as a mouse –
a *biscuit* figure fled the house!

"Sis – run!" it yelled. "Fast as you can!"
"*Hansel?*" Goldy screamed, then RAN!
She fled the house and jumped a ditch.
The old hag must have been a witch!

Poor Goldy sprinted through the night.
She ran and ran till morning light.
But then a sweet smell filled the air.
"The witch!" cried Goldy in despair.

But no, it wasn't gingerbread –
for when she turned she saw instead
a handsome cottage roofed with thatch.
Its door was even off the latch…

She knocked – but then began to choke,
for – crumbs! – the house was filled
  with smoke!
"*Fire!* Someone help!" she cried,
then held her breath and ran inside.

There on the stove she found a hot
and bubbling-over porridge-pot!
She quenched the flames and cleared
  the smoke,
then put the dirty pot to soak.

"I wonder who could own this home?"
thought Goldilocks. "Some elves? A gnome?
Of *course* – the *dwarves*! They couldn't
cook!
Snow White cared for them in the book!"

Then Goldy had a great idea –
"If I wash up, and cook, and clear,
perhaps the dwarves will let *me* stay,
and even help me find my way!"

So Goldy quickly grabbed a broom
and washed and swept and scrubbed
  the room…

Then cooked more oats and stirred
  them well.
Her tummy rumbled at the smell.

She took a bite – "Too *sour*!" she cried.
She grabbed the sugar from the side,
and tried again. "Now it's too *sweet*!
My teeth are rotting as I eat!"

She added water, salt and spice,
then cinnamon that smelled so nice.

She mixed in apples, grapes, sultanas,
chocolate drops and ripe bananas...

Everything went in the pot.
She mixed it up and stirred a lot,
then held her breath and took a bite...
"At last," she cried. "That tastes *just right*!"

She licked her lips – it tasted dreamy!
Smooth and rich and oh-so-creamy!
"Yum!" she grinned. "Just *one* more spoon!"
She ate and ate till very soon...

…the pot was bare – so was the box!
"There's no oats left!" wailed Goldilocks.

She searched and searched, then with a sigh
she saw the spare box – way up high…

"Too *high*!" cried Goldy in despair –
and then she spied a wooden chair.
She pushed and pulled and shoved
    and nudged –
but still the big chair wouldn't budge!

"It's just too *heavy*!" Goldy cried.
She tried the next – "Too *soft*!" she sighed.

The smallest chair turned out *just right*.
She climbed on top – the perfect height!

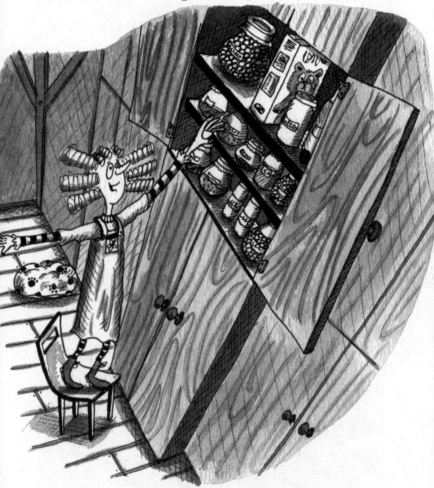

She stretched her hand towards the box –
but then – oh no! – poor Goldilocks…

The porridge scattered everywhere
as Goldy fell – and broke the chair!

"Oh crumbs!" she wailed. "Look at
this mess!
The chair! The floor! Oh no – my *dress*!
I can't meet dwarves with stains
and splatter –
first impressions really matter!"

She rushed upstairs to clean her frock.
She turned the tap – and got a shock!

The water soaked her through and through!
"Oh no!" she wailed, then sneezed –
   "ATCHOO!"

"What now?" she cried. "I'm cold,
    I'm tired,
my plan has totally backfired.
I've lost my brother, lost my way,
and now they'll never let me stay!"

She flopped down on the nearest bed.
But, "Ouch!" It was as hard as *lead*!

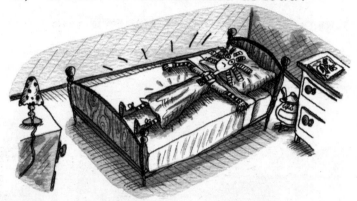

She tried the next – but it was *lumpy*!
All the springs were stiff and *bumpy*!

"Ugh," she sighed, then tried bed three,
which was as comfy as could be!
Poor Goldy yawned, and curled up tight –
she hadn't slept at all that night.

"Just forty winks…" She snuggled down
beneath the fluffy eiderdown.
She closed her eyes, began to snore.
But then, all of a sudden…

...ROAR!

Three BEARS burst through the
bedroom door!

"You're not dwarves!" poor Goldy howled.
"No kidding, thief!" the big bear growled.

"You broke our chair and ate our food,
and slept in all our beds? How rude!"
He roared, "I'll teach you not to steal –
you'll make us all a lovely meal!"

"Oh, please don't eat me!" Goldy cried.
She fled the room and raced outside.

The big bear sighed, "Well, what a fuss!
I just meant she should cook for us!"

Poor Goldy raced between the trees.
"Oh someone, somewhere, help me, please!"
She found a house, banged on the door.
"Please let me in!" she begged, then saw…

A *wolf* was sleeping in the bed!
Poor Goldy gasped – and then she fled!

The sky grew dark and lightning flashed,
the rain poured down and thunder crashed.
Then – gleaming in the lightning's light –
she saw a castle in the night!

She rushed up to the iron gate.
"Please help!" she cried. "I know it's late!"

"Of course, my dear," a woman said.
And led her to the *strangest* bed...

For *forty* mattresses in all
were stacked up high against the wall!

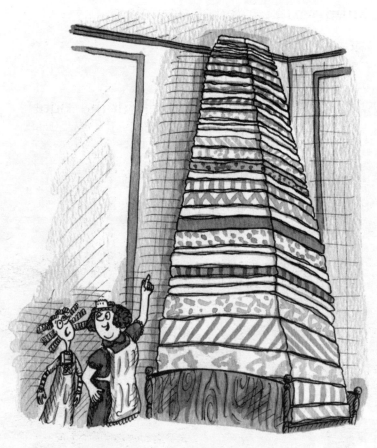

Young Goldy's jaw dropped at the sight.
"Goodnight," the woman grinned.
"Sleep tight!"

Poor Goldy climbed the giant heap.
But though exhausted, couldn't sleep.
A lump was keeping her awake:
it made her little body ache.

She tossed and turned throughout the night
till finally the sky grew light.
A maid burst in. "The queen is here!
She wants to meet you – hurry, dear!"

"Alas, my child, you look so tired.

Did you sleep well?" the queen enquired.

"No, not a wink," poor Goldy sighed.

"A lump kept digging in my side."

"How wonderful!" Her Highness cried.

"Quick, call the prince – we've found
    his bride!"

"The prince's bride? What do you mean?"
"You found the pea!" rejoiced the queen.
"*What* pea? *Where?*" young Goldy said.
"My dear, the pea within your bed!"

"You see there is a prophecy:
'Our *true* princess will feel the pea!'
I've tested lots of girls – none passed,
till you, dear – our princess – at last!"

42

It didn't take much to convince
young Goldilocks to wed the prince!

At last she found herself well placed
to use her undisputed taste:
she oversaw the palace cooks…

…wrote tasty homemade cookery-books…

…designed a range of beds and chairs
(and sent free samples to the bears).

She found her brother, lived her dream –
they dined on caviar and cream…

But never once forgot the pea –
she put it somewhere all could see.
A message to all future queens:
always be thankful for your greens!

Fairy Tale Twists

Written by Katie Dale
Illustrated by Matt Buckingham

The Big Bad Werewolf	978 1 40831 218 6
Goldilocks and the Pea	978 1 40831 219 3
The Not-So-Evil Stepmother	978 1 40831 220 9
The Wickedest Witch	978 1 40831 221 6
Prince Charming's Princess Quest	978 1 40831 222 3
The Unfair-y Godmother	978 1 40831 223 0
Jack to the Rescue!	978 1 40831 224 7
Three Magic Mice	978 1 40831 225 4

All priced at £4.99

Orchard Books are available from all good bookshops,
or can be ordered from our website, www.orchardbooks.co.uk,
or telephone 01235 827702, or fax 01235 827703.